Can you help me tidy up, please? And look for the cheeky little bears. They always hide at bedtime.

Fork

Jar

Just look at the kitchen! Someone has left things on the floor. Can you point to where they belong?

Plate

Cereal

Mug

Carrots

Eggs

Frying
pan

Thank you. Did you hear that noise?

I think little Lily bear is hiding. Can you see her and can you find her red toy car?

Apples

Picture

Look at the living room!
Can you put these things
away, please?

Goldfish

Books

Newspaper

Cushion

Lampshade

That's better. Now can you find Jack bear and tell him it's nearly bedtime?

He'll want his toy aeroplane.
Can you see it anywhere?

Glove

Balls

Umbrella

Hello! Now we are in the hall. Let's put these things away.

Boot

Keys

Flowers

Coat

I think little Evie bear is hiding in here somewhere.

Where do you think she is? And can
you see her toy boat?

Flowerpots

Paintbrush

Bucket

Screwdriver

The garage is a mess, too. Can you help us put these things away?

Spanner

Watering
can

Saw

Thank you. It's getting late now.

Where is Harry bear? I think he's hiding in here, and where is his green toy tractor?

Showercap

Here we are in the bathroom
and there are more things
to put away.

Toothbrush

Toilet roll

Towel

Duck

Flannel

Hairbrush

Well done. We've found Jack, Lily, Evie and Harry but we still have to find one more little bear.

Can you see Olivia bear? And where is her space rocket?

At last the little bears are ready for bed.

Can you put each bear into the right bed please, and give each one the right mug from my tray?

Goodnight, little bears. Now I can go downstairs and read my book.

Oh dear, where did I put my glasses?
Can you see them anywhere?

What a busy time we've had! Thank you for helping me.
I do hope you'll come and visit us again soon.